A Christmas Journey with the Purple Crayon

Harold at
the North Pole

by Crockett Johnson

FOUNTAINDALE PUBLIC LIBRARY DISTRICT
300 West Briarcliff Road
Bolingbrook, IL 60440-2894
(630) 759-2102

📖 HarperCollins*Publishers*

This story was first published, in a somewhat abbreviated version, in GOOD HOUSEKEEPING

It was Christmas Eve, and Harold had to have
a Christmas tree before Santa Claus arrived.

So, in a warm woolen cap and mittens, with his purple crayon and the moon, he set off for the north woods.

Harold made sure he went north, by the big dipper. He was glad it happened to be a clear starry night.

Suddenly he remembered Santa Claus came
by sleigh. There would have to be snow.

And there was snow. There was a blizzard.

Harold shivered. It's a fine night to be out,
he thought, for a snowman.

The snowstorm was worse than he imagined.
Even a snowman didn't look cheerful in it.

Harold gave the snowman a muffler to wear.

And, happily, the storm finally was showing
signs of letting up.

The snow stopped falling but it lay in big
drifts. It covered everything.

From the looks of things, Harold thought, he might very well be at the North Pole.

But this couldn't be really the North Pole,
he told himself, because he knew that Santa
Claus's workshop is at the North Pole.

And here all Harold could see was snow.

Still, it did look remarkably like the North
Pole, Harold reflected, as he climbed up on
a snowdrift as big as a house.

It was a house. He really was at the North
Pole, on the roof of Santa's workshop.

With smooth snow over the eaves Harold was
sure Santa Claus was inside. He was snowed
in. And it was the night before Christmas.

Why, Harold asked excitedly, couldn't Santa
come out up the chimney?

Then he realized that was a silly question.

Of course Santa Claus could come up a chimney.

The difficulty was, Santa's sleigh full of toys
couldn't come out that way. Harold thought.

Then he acted fast. He told Santa to come
out without the sleigh and not to worry, to
leave things to him.

Santa Claus appeared to be rather doubtful.

But Harold confidently went to work lining
up the reindeer.

Soon Prancer and Dancer were pawing at the
snow, eager to be off around the world.

Harold wasn't quite certain of the names of
the other reindeer.

But he made sure there were eight of them.

They were all handsome and spirited animals.

And, if they weren't exactly in their right order, none of them complained.

Harold harnessed them with no difficulty.

And he hitched them to a splendid sleigh.

It had a comfortable seat for Santa Claus.

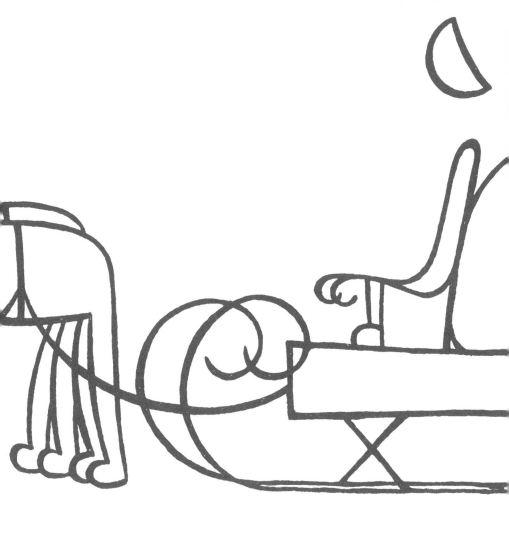

And it had room for a sizeable bag of toys.

He generously filled the bag to overflowing.

For a moment Harold thought of looking to
see which were his presents.

But there wasn't time. He told Santa Claus
to get in the sleigh and deliver the toys.

And, without more ado, he waved goodbye.

He would have liked to ride with Santa but
he still had to find a Christmas tree.

And he had to get it home, and decorate it too, before Santa got there.

He looked everywhere for a Christmas tree,
but all he could see was the moon.

He wondered how the moon would look on top of a Christmas tree, as an ornament.

It looked fine over the tree. And the tree
also looked fine under the moon.

It was just the tree he had been looking for.
Now the only problem was to get it home.

It had to stand in the living room, between
the fireplace and the big soft chair.

Fortunately, the tree fitted in perfectly.

Harold hung up one of his stockings on the
fireplace mantel.

And he climbed into the big soft chair to
wait for Santa Claus to arrive.